Fall Is for Friends

Suzy Spafford

SCHOLASTIC INC.

New York   Toronto   London   Auckland   Sydney
Mexico City   New Delhi   Hong Kong   Buenos Aires

For Kerstyn and Jennifer

Copyright © 2003 by Suzy Spafford.
All rights reserved. Published by Scholastic Inc.
SCHOLASTIC, CARTWHEEL BOOKS, and associated logos are trademarks and/or registered trademarks of Scholastic Inc.
Suzy's Zoo, Suzy Ducken, and associated logos and character designs are trademarks and service marks of Suzy's Zoo in the United States and other countries.

ISBN 0-439-40185-2
Reinforced Binding for Library Use
Library of Congress Cataloging-in-Publication Data is available.

10 9 8 7 6 5 4 3 2 1   03 04 05 06 07

Printed in Mexico 49
First printing, October 2003

Suzy Ducken loved everything about fall. She loved wrapping herself in big, cozy sweaters. She loved crisp apples and big orange pumpkins.

But most of all, she loved jumping into piles of leaves with her best friend, Emily. Until they took that first running leap every year, it didn't feel as if fall had really arrived.

"When are the leaves going to fall?" Suzy wondered.
"Maybe they just need a little help!" declared Emily.

Suzy had never thought of that.
"You mean we could help the leaves
fall off the trees?" she asked Emily.

"Of course!" her friend said confidently.
"This is *us* we're talking about!"

Now all that the girls had to do was figure out how to get the leaves to drop. They needed a plan.

They had so many ideas. Back in Suzy's room, they piled all the things they might need into a big cardboard box.

First Suzy and Emily tried leading a cheer to make the leaves *want* to fall from the trees.

"Fall, leaves, fall!
That's what we say.
Hit the ground,
so we can play!"

When that didn't work, Emily said, "Maybe we should *show* the leaves what fun it would be to fall."

So the friends set to work cutting leaf shapes out of construction paper and taping them all over each other.

"Let's show them how it's done!" Emily said. The two girls began to dance and spin among the trees.

"Oh, how I love to ride a gentle breeze and fall softly to the ground," Emily said in a dreamy voice.

Emily quickly became so dizzy that she actually did fall — but it wasn't softly.

"I am floating! I am free!" trilled Suzy, tripping over Emily.

This time Suzy tried a little magic.
"Leaves of brilliant red and gold,
fall before we both grow old!" she commanded.

The leaves stayed right where they were.

As the friends wondered what to do next, Emily
began to hum a tune. Emily always hummed when she
was concentrating especially hard.

"That's it!" shouted Suzy suddenly. "We'll *sing* the
leaves off the trees!"

"Songs can help you think. Songs can make you happy. Some songs can make you want to get up and dance," Suzy continued. "So why can't a song make the leaves want to fall off the trees?"

"Well, what are we waiting for?" asked Emily. "Let's make up a fall song!"

A little while later, the girls joined hands,
took deep breaths, and sang:

Blow, breeze, blow the leaves,
gently to the ground.
My friend and I are waiting!
And fall is all around!

"We did it!" the girls whispered
to each other in amazement.

Now it felt like fall!